First Facts®

Positively Pets

Caring for Your
Ferret

by Kathy Feeney

Consultant:
Jennifer Zablotny, DVM
Member, American Veterinary Medical Association

Capstone
press®

Mankato, Minnesota

First Facts is published by Capstone Press,
151 Good Counsel Drive, P.O. Box 669, Mankato, Minnesota 56002.
www.capstonepress.com

Library of Congress Cataloging-in-Publication Data
Feeney, Kathy, 1954–
    Caring for your ferret/by Kathy Feeney.
    p. cm. — (First facts. Positively pets)
    Summary: "Describes caring for a ferret, including supplies needed, feeding, cleaning, health,
safety, and aging" — Provided by publisher.
    Includes bibliographical references and index.
    ISBN-13: 978-1-4296-1253-1 (hardcover)
    ISBN-10: 1-4296-1253-3 (hardcover)
    1. Ferrets as pets — Juvenile literature. I. Title. II. Series.
SF459.F47F44 2008
636.976'628 — dc22   2007030365

Editorial Credits
Gillia Olson, editor; Bobbi J. Wyss, set designer; Kyle Grenz, book designer and illustrator;
    Kelly Garvin, photo researcher/photo stylist

Photo Credits
All photos Capstone Press/Karon Dubke, except page 20, iStockphoto/AtWaG

Capstone Press thanks Pet Expo and River Hills Pet Care Hospital in Mankato, Minnesota, and
    Nancy White of North Mankato, Minnesota, for assistance with photo shoots for this book.

1 2 3 4 5 6 13 12 11 10 09 08

Table of Contents

Do You Want a Ferret?

    Ferrets are furry, friendly, and funny. They tumble around, play with toys, and can even learn tricks.

    But owning a ferret is a big job. Your pet will depend on you for food, water, and safety. Are you ready for this **responsibility**?

I have a natural musky odor. It's worse if I still have my scent glands. Check if I've had these glands removed before you buy me.

Supplies to Buy

You can buy a home for your ferret at a pet store. Choose a tall cage with two or more levels. Place a litter box in the cage. You can train your ferret to use it. Line the rest of the floor with cloth cage pads to protect your ferret's feet. Your pet will also need food, a water bottle, and **bedding**.

You might want to buy a leash too. You can teach me to walk with one.

Your Ferret at Home

Ferrets are loving and friendly. Talk to your new pet softly, and pick it up gently. You'll become great friends.

Ferrets get along great with other ferrets. But be careful around other pets. Cats and dogs can hurt ferrets. Your ferret could hurt pet mice or hamsters.

Ferrets enjoy roaming your home. Keep an eye on them. Ferrets can get hurt. They may chew on wires. They may be stepped on when they hide under a rug.

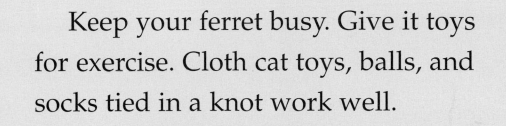

Keep your ferret busy. Give it toys for exercise. Cloth cat toys, balls, and socks tied in a knot work well.

Cleaning

Ferrets stay clean. They don't need baths very often. But you will need to keep your ferret's ears clean. You will also need to trim your ferret's nails.

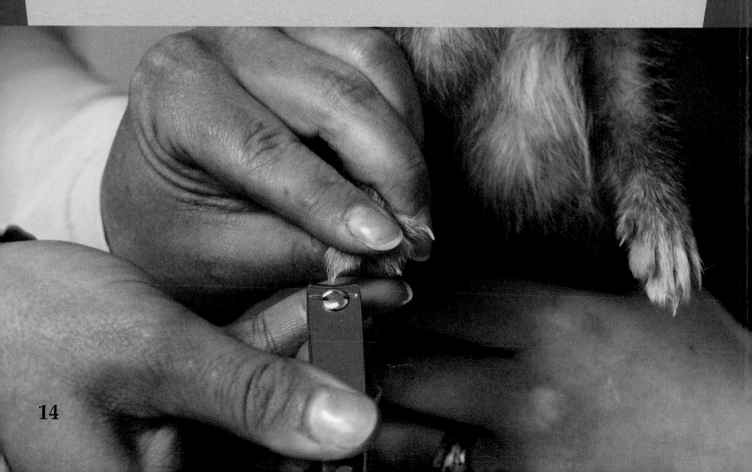

You must keep your ferret's cage
clean. Dirty cages can make ferrets
sick. Take out dirty bedding every day.
Change the litter box often.

Ferret Health

Before you buy a ferret, check if it is **spayed** or **neutered**. These operations stop animals from having babies. Females must be spayed for health reasons.

If they are sick, ferrets will usually stop eating and playing. A **veterinarian** can check your pet to make sure it is healthy.

Your Ferret's Life

Most ferrets live six to eight years. You and your ferret can have lots of fun together. Just make sure your ferret gets plenty of exercise and has a clean home. As your ferret gets older, it will slow down a little. But ferrets remain playful their whole lives.

Wild Relatives!

Some people think ferrets are rodents, but they aren't. Your ferret is related to the otter, polecat, weasel, mink, and skunk. Another relative, the black-footed ferret, is in danger of dying out. All of these animals are furry with long bodies, short legs, and pointed faces.

polecat

Decode Your Ferret's Behavior

- Ferrets are deep sleepers. If you can't wake up your ferret, don't worry. Just make sure your ferret is warm and breathing.

- Ferrets don't have good eyesight. They often bump into things.

- The name ferret means thief. Ferrets like to steal and hide car keys, watches, and food. In the wild, ferrets gather and store things to line their dens.

- Ferrets cluck like chickens when they are happy.

- If you hear a screech, your ferret is hurt, frightened, or angry.

Glossary

bedding (BED-ing) — material used to make a bed; use cloth or old towels for ferret bedding.

carnivore (KAHR-nuh-vohr) — an animal that eats only meat

neuter (NOO-tur) — to operate on a male animal so it is unable to produce young

protein (PROH-teen) — a substance found in foods such as meat, cheese, eggs, and fish

responsibility (ri-spon-suh-BIL-uh-tee) — a duty or a job

spay (SPAY) — to operate on a female animal so it is unable to produce young

veterinarian (vet-ur-uh-NER-ee-uhn) — a doctor who treats sick or injured animals; veterinarians also help animals stay healthy.

Read More

Doudna, Kelly. *Frisky Ferrets*. Perfect Pets. Edina, Minn.: Abdo, 2007.

Hamilton, Lynn. *Caring for Your Ferret*. Caring for Your Pet. New York: Weigl, 2004.

Waters, Jo. *The Wild Side of Pet Ferrets*. Raintree Perspectives. Chicago: Raintree, 2005.

Internet Sites

FactHound offers a safe, fun way to find Internet sites related to this book. All of the sites on FactHound have been researched by our staff.

Here's how:

1. Visit *www.facthound.com*

2. Choose your grade level.

3. Type in this book ID **1429612533** for age-appropriate sites. You may also browse subjects by clicking on letters, or by clicking on pictures and words.

4. Click on the **Fetch It** button.

FactHound will fetch the best sites for you!

Index